MAX ★★★ for ★★★ President

★ Jarrett J. ★ Krosoczka ★

Alfred A. Knopf • New York

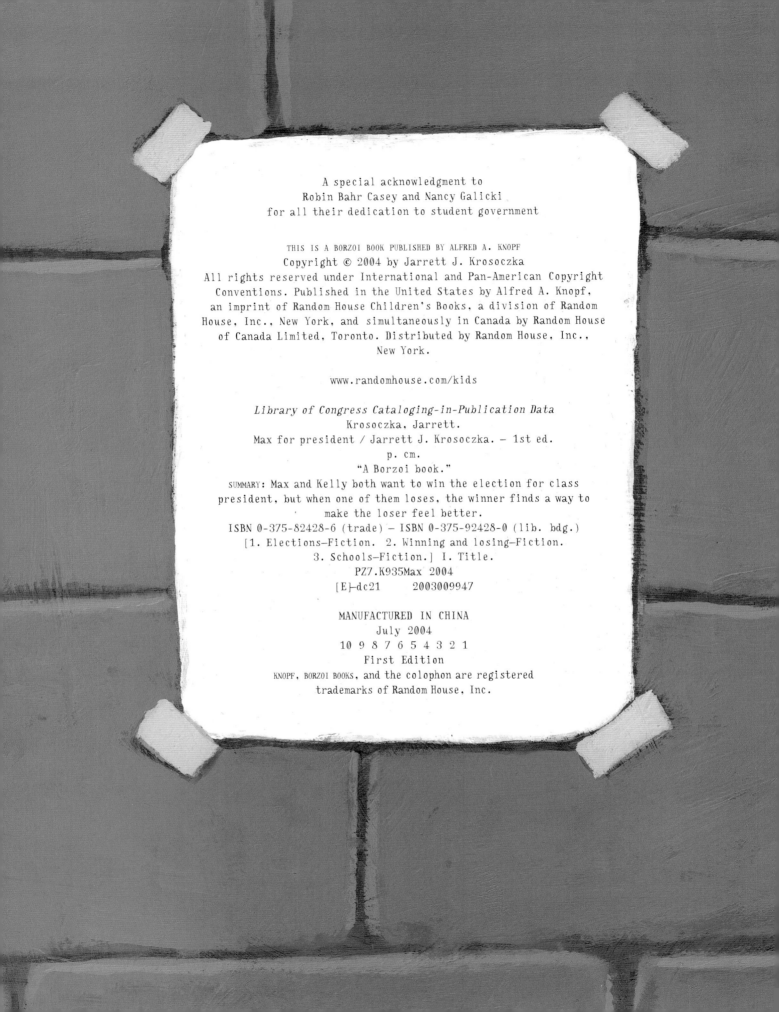

A special acknowledgment to
Robin Bahr Casey and Nancy Galicki
for all their dedication to student government

THIS IS A BORZOI BOOK PUBLISHED BY ALFRED A. KNOPF
Copyright © 2004 by Jarrett J. Krosoczka
All rights reserved under International and Pan-American Copyright
Conventions. Published in the United States by Alfred A. Knopf,
an imprint of Random House Children's Books, a division of Random
House, Inc., New York, and simultaneously in Canada by Random House
of Canada Limited, Toronto. Distributed by Random House, Inc.,
New York.

www.randomhouse.com/kids

Library of Congress Cataloging-in-Publication Data
Krosoczka, Jarrett.
Max for president / Jarrett J. Krosoczka. — 1st ed.
p. cm.
"A Borzoi book."
SUMMARY: Max and Kelly both want to win the election for class
president, but when one of them loses, the winner finds a way to
make the loser feel better.
ISBN 0-375-82428-6 (trade) — ISBN 0-375-92428-0 (lib. bdg.)
[1. Elections—Fiction. 2. Winning and losing—Fiction.
3. Schools—Fiction.] I. Title.
PZ7.K935Max 2004
[E]—dc21   2003009947

MANUFACTURED IN CHINA
July 2004
10 9 8 7 6 5 4 3 2 1
First Edition
KNOPF, BORZOI BOOKS, and the colophon are registered
trademarks of Random House, Inc.

Mrs. Antonio announced that it was time to elect a new class president.

MAX thought that he would like to be class president.

So did
KELLY.

Max made signs that said

"Max for President."

FOR
LLY
school
for
belly!
VOTE FOR
KELLY
Better school
lunches for
your belly!

Kelly made signs, too.

Max made buttons and gave them
to all of his classmates.

So did Kelly.

Max made promises.

Kelly made promises, too.

The time came to vote. Every
student could only vote
for one candidate—
Max or Kelly!

Max waited anxiously.

So did Kelly.

After the ballots were collected and counted, Mrs. Antonio announced the winner.

Kelly cheered.

Max didn't.

Kelly knew that she needed a good vice president to help get work done. She thought for a second and then asked . . .

And from then on, both Kelly and Max worked hard to make their school a better place.

The End